Karen's Prize

Karen's Prize

ANN M. MARTIN

ILLUSTRATIONS BY HEATHER BURNS

SCHOLASTIC INC.

The author gratefully acknowledges
Stephanie Calmenson for her
help with this book.

Copyright © 1990 by Ann M. Martin

This book was originally published in paperback in 1990.

All rights reserved. Published by Scholastic Inc., *Publishers since 1920.* SCHOLASTIC, BABY-SITTERS LITTLE SISTER, and associated logos are trademarks and/or registered trademarks of Scholastic Inc.

ISBN 978-1-338-81509-2

10 9 8 7 6 5 4 3 2 1   22 23 24 25 26

Printed in the U.S.A. 40
This edition first printing 2022

Book design by Maeve Norton

CHAPTER 1

Last one to her seat is a rotten egg!" I called.

I am Karen Brewer. I am seven years old and in second grade at Stoneybrook Academy. I was racing with Nancy and Hannie, my best friends. We are in the same class at school. We call ourselves the Three Musketeers.

I reached my seat first.

"I won!" I shouted.

"Indoor voice, please," said my teacher, Ms. Colman.

Ms. Colman is *won*derful. If you have a question, she answers it without making you feel dumb. She never yells. And even if she scolds you sometimes, like now, you know she still likes you.

Ms. Colman has to remind me to use my indoor voice a lot. That is because I forget a lot. I was about to forget one more time.

After attendance, Ms. Colman said, "Today is Wednesday. Next Monday, we will have a spelling bee in class."

That is when I shouted again. "Hurray!"

Ms. Colman was not pleased. "Indoor voice, Karen. And please don't interrupt."

I could hardly wait to hear about the spelling bee, so I made believe I was buttoning my lips. Ms. Colman smiled.

"This is going to be a very special spelling bee," continued Ms. Colman. "It will be the first of many spelling bees in the next few weeks. Whoever wins the spelling bee in our class will go on to compete with other winners in grades one, two, and three. The winners of those contests will face the winners in other schools in Stoneybrook. Then there will be another contest for the best spellers in each county, and finally *those* winners will go on to a contest at our state capital. The winner of that contest will be declared the best junior speller in the whole state of Connecticut."

I hoped Ms. Colman was finished, because I could not keep quiet one single minute longer.

"Wow!" I burst out. I was not the only one talking now. The whole room was buzzing — like bees!

All I could think about the rest of the morning was the spelling bee. I am a great speller and I *love* contests.

When recess came I pulled my hopscotch stone out of my desk and headed for the playground with Hannie and Nancy.

It was my turn to go first. I threw the stone. It landed on the third square. "H-O-P!" I spelled, as I hopped across the squares.

"Aren't you excited about the spelling bee?" I asked when I finished.

"It will be fun," said Hannie, throwing the stone.

"We're all good spellers," said Nancy.

"What do you mean, good? We're grrreat!" I shouted. (At recess I am allowed to use my outdoor voice.)

We were pretty excited. So were most of the other kids. Except for Pamela Harding. But that was no surprise. She does not like much of anything. I found that out when I invited her to my sleepover. She would not sleep in a sleeping bag (she said she *has* to sleep in a bed). She would not eat pizza (she says it gives her bad breath). She did not even like *The Wizard of Oz*!

"I couldn't care less about a baby spelling bee. I hate contests," Pamela said.

Jannie Gilbert looked like she thought Pamela might be right.

But not me. I did not care what Pamela said. I was going to be the best junior speller in the state of Connecticut!

CHAPTER 2

After school I studied my spelling book. There were lots of food words. *Potato. Banana. Cookie.*

I decided to skip those words for now. I did not want to get hungry. Then I would have to get up for a snack. Then I would not be studying my spelling words!

I found a word that wouldn't make me hungry. *Family.*

I looked through my book. It was only there one time. If they knew anything about *my* family they would have listed it twice.

That is because I am a two-two. Karen Two-Two. That is what I call myself because of my two families. I got the name from a book Ms. Colman read to our class. It was called *Jacob*

Two-Two Meets the Hooded Fang. I am not the only one who is a two-two. My brother, Andrew, who is four, is a two-two, too!

This is what happened. A long time ago my mommy and daddy got divorced. Then they married other people. Mommy married Seth. Now he is our stepfather. Most of the time Andrew and I (and Emily Junior, my rat) live with Mommy and Seth in the little house. That is where I am now. Since there are just four of us, a little house is fine.

"Mrr-ow!" Oh, right. I forgot about Rocky, Seth's cat. He was rubbing against my leg right that very minute. And there is Midgie, Seth's dog. But Rocky and Midgie do not take up much room.

Every other weekend, and for two weeks in the summer, Andrew and I go to the big house. And I mean *big*. It is a mansion! That is because Daddy is a millionaire. Daddy married Elizabeth. Now she's our stepmother. She has four kids.

There are Sam and Charlie. They are old. They are in high school.

There is Kristy. She is thirteen. She is my favorite, favorite person. She baby-sits for Andrew and me and lots of other kids. You know what? She has her own business. It is called the Baby-sitters Club and Kristy is the president.

David Michael is just a little bit older than I am. Sometimes he can be a pain.

Emily Michelle is my little sister. She is two years old. She was born in a country called Vietnam. (I love her so I named my rat after her.)

And Nannie, Elizabeth's mother, is my

stepgrandmother. She came to live in the big house to help take care of Emily Michelle. But she really helps everyone. She is pretty neat.

That's a lot of people, isn't it? Plus there is Shannon. She is a Bernese mountain dog puppy. She is David Michael's dog. And Boo-Boo is Daddy's fat, mostly mean, old cat.

Part of being a two-two means having two of lots of things. I usually get to have two birthday parties. I have two pairs of pink sneakers, two pairs of jeans, and two stuffed cats (Goosie at the little house and Moosie at the big house). I even have two pieces of Tickly, my special blanket. I had to rip Tickly in half to have two pieces, but I'm sure it only hurt for a second.

Uh-oh. I am supposed to be studying my spelling words. I am not supposed to be daydreaming.

Family. F-A-M-I-L-Y.

CHAPTER 3

I love waking up in my room at the big house. It was Saturday, so I did not have to hurry out of bed. But I knew there would be lots going on when I did.

"Good morning, M-O-O-S-I-E. Good morning, T-I-C-K-L-Y," I said.

I heard people laughing downstairs. I did not want to miss out on anything fun. So I got dressed fast and ran to the kitchen.

Everyone was sitting around the table, having breakfast.

"Hi, Karen!" said Kristy. She gave me a great big hug.

I sat down next to her and poured myself

a bowl of Krispy Krunchy cereal. I sliced a B-A-N-A-N-A on top.

"Who's going to help me with my spelling words?" I asked.

"We gave you about a million words last night," said Sam. "But, wait, here's one more. G-O-O-D-B-Y-E spells good-bye!" Sam got up and left. Sam likes to tease.

"What do you have to practice so much for, Professor?" asked David Michael.

When I got my glasses, David Michael started calling me Professor. He was not being mean. But now I could tell he was teasing.

"I don't *have* to practice," I said. "I could win the spelling bee anyway. But Ms. Colman said we should."

"I'd help you, Karen. But I have a special Baby-sitters Club meeting," said Kristy. "You can study in my room, though."

"Thanks!" I said. I knew that I would feel very grown-up in Kristy's room.

After breakfast, I got my spelling book. Then I went to find Daddy. He was in the garden, pulling weeds.

"Would you help me now, Daddy?" I asked.

"Karen, honey, you know I can't hold your spelling book and pull weeds at the same time," he said. "I'll help you practice tonight."

Gee. You would think the spelling bee did not matter. And I had told everybody that if I won this contest, I would get to be in the next one and the next and the next and the next till I was the state champion!

I decided to go to Kristy's room and make flash cards with my spelling words on them. I cut up pieces of paper. I took my red marker and wrote one word on each card.

Then I went back down to the garden.

"Okay, Daddy. Now you don't have to hold a book. I'll hold up a card. You just say the word," I told him.

Daddy sighed. He did not seem too happy. "I

will give you three words. That is all for now," he said.

He gave me three words. Then I went to find Elizabeth. She was changing Emily Michelle's diaper.

"Please, please, please! Just three words. Daddy gave me three," I said.

"All right. Three words," said Elizabeth. Emily Michelle started crying, so I only got to spell two words.

That was not bad, though. Charlie and Nannie each gave me a few more words. Then I went up to Kristy's room again.

I found her English book. There were lots of words in there that I knew. And she is in *eighth* grade! Of course I had to tell everyone. What is the fun of being smart if no one knows?

At dinner I announced, "I can spell geometry! G-E-O-M-E-T-R-Y."

"Big deal," said David Michael.

"Okay, smarty-pants. Here's one for you," I said. "Spell *sincerely.*"

"Um, S-I-N-um-S —" said David Michael.

"Wrong! It's S-I-N-C-E-R-E-L-Y!" I shouted. "You're older than I am and you can't even spell *sincerely*!"

"Karen, chill out," said Charlie.

Charlie's usually nice to me. If *he* said to chill out, he must be serious.

For the next five minutes I practiced by myself.

CHAPTER 4

It was Monday! It was the day of our class spelling bee. Mommy drove me and Nancy Dawes to school in the morning. We took turns spelling words in the car.

"Good luck, girls," Mommy said when we reached school. She blew us both kisses.

"All right, class. Settle down," said Ms. Colman a little later on. "We are going to have our spelling bee right after attendance. When I call your name, I want you to line up at the side of the room. Ready? Karen Brewer."

"Here!" I answered. I wanted to say "Here I am, the next Junior Champion Speller!" But I did not. I just grabbed my strawberry eraser and slipped it in my pocket for good luck.

When we were all lined up, Ms. Colman explained how the spelling bee worked.

"I will give you a word. You say the word, spell it, then say it again. If you spell the word correctly, I will ask you to walk to the end of the line. If you make a mistake, I will ask you to sit down at your desk. You may do crossword puzzles, read, or talk quietly. And, remember, making a mistake is not a terrible thing. It is easy to forget a word, or to get nervous."

A few kids asked questions. Ricky Torres asked how long we had to spell a word. Ms. Colman just said we should not take all day.

Then the contest started. I got to go first.

"Karen, please spell *apple*," said Ms. Colman.

Boy, was I lucky. That was easy!

"Apple. A-P-P-L-E. Apple," I said.

"That is correct," said Ms. Colman. "You may go to the end of the line."

I took a few bows, then skipped to the end.

"Let's not get carried away," said Ms. Colman. "Walking will be fine."

Three more kids spelled words right. Then Leslie Morris made a mistake. She put an extra *n* in *banana* and had to go to her seat.

Soon there were a bunch of kids sitting down. Pamela and Jannie. Even Hannie and Ricky Torres had missed their words.

But nobody was doing puzzles, or anything. Except Pamela. She was reading a book. Everyone else was watching. And it was my turn, so they were watching *me!*

"Karen, your next word is *igloo*," said Ms. Colman.

"What a great word! Igloo. I-G-L-O-O. Igloo. Brrr!" I said.

Ms. Colman sent me to the end of the line. Hurray!

The next word was *noisy*. I could not believe it. Three kids got it wrong! Then guess who was left? Just me and Nancy. It was my turn.

"Noisy. N-O-I-S-Y. Noisy," I said.

"That is correct," said Ms. Colman.

Everyone started jumping up and down.

"Calm down, girls. We're not finished," said Ms. Colman. She gave me and Nancy more words. We kept getting them right.

"The next one is for you, Nancy," said Ms. Colman. "Please spell *hurricane*."

"Hurricane. H-E-R-R-I-C-A-N-E. Hurricane," said Nancy.

"I'm sorry. That is not correct," said Ms. Colman.

Poor Nancy. I knew she just got careless.

That was one of the words Mommy gave us in the car. And Nancy had spelled it right then.

"Karen, if you can spell *hurricane* right, you are our class winner," said Ms. Colman.

I wanted to make sure everyone could hear me. In my almost outdoor voice, I said, "Hurricane. H-U-R-R-I-C-A-N-E. Hurricane!"

Then I started jumping up and down. I knew — I just *knew* — I had gotten it right.

The rest of the class knew, too. Almost everyone was clapping like crazy! Except for Pamela. She just turned a page in her book. I bet she was jealous.

Guess what happened then! I got a prize. Ms. Colman gave me a copy of a book called *The Phantom Tollbooth*.

"Congratulations, Karen," said Ms. Colman. "Next Monday, you will compete against the other first-, second-, and third-grade winners in our school."

Wow! I won! I really won! I could hardly wait to get home and tell everybody.

CHAPTER 5

D o I look the same as I did this morning?" I asked Mommy and Andrew when they picked me up at school. "Well, I'm not!" I said before they had a chance to answer. "I am now the winner of my class spelling bee!"

"Hurray!" said Andrew.

"That is wonderful!" said Mommy. "I am proud of you."

"I even won a prize," I said. I showed them my book.

At home, I gobbled up my snack. (I was gigundo hungry.)

"Mommy, I'm going to Nancy's house!" I called. Nancy lives next door to Mommy.

I could not wait to tell Mrs. Dawes about the spelling bee.

But she already knew. Nancy told her. "That's great, Karen!" said Mrs. Dawes. "Nancy! Karen's here."

I went to Nancy's room. She had made a big blue ribbon for me.

"Wow! What a great best friend," I said. "We need to give you a red ribbon for being the runner-up."

"Nah. I gave myself a blue one, too. Only it's a little smaller," said Nancy.

We started giggling and buzzing like bees because we were the best spellers in the class!

When I got back home, I asked Mommy if I could make a few phone calls before I studied. (Ms. Colman had given me a long list of new words.) Mommy said yes.

First I called the big house. I wanted everyone there to know, especially Daddy and Kristy. And David Michael, because he thinks he is so smart. And Sam and Charlie. And —

Ring! Ring!

Kristy answered. Hurray!

"Hi, Kristy! It's Karen. You want to know what happened today? I won the spelling bee!" I said.

Kristy was really proud. She promised to tell Daddy and everyone else. I knew I could count on Kristy.

Then I called all of my grandmas and

grandpas. (I have a lot of them.) I was thinking about who to call next when Seth came home.

I almost knocked him down in the doorway.

"I won! I won!" I said.

"Mommy told me! That's terrific!" said Seth.

While Seth was washing up, I asked him to give me words to spell.

While he and Mommy were making dinner, I told them they could take turns giving me more words.

And at dinner, when Seth asked me to pass the potatoes, I said, "Only if you give me a word first."

"Let's take a break now, Karen," said Seth.

"How do you play a spelling bee?" asked Andrew.

"What a dumb question," I said. "It isn't a game."

"Karen, that wasn't nice," said Mommy. "Please apologize."

"Apologize!" I said. "That's on my list. A-P-O-L-O —"

"Please answer your brother's question," said Seth.

"A spelling bee is when everyone lines up and gets to spell words," I said.

"Which words?" asked Andrew.

"The words on the list the teacher gives you. But that doesn't matter. All that matters is that I'm going to be the best junior speller in the state of Connecticut. C-O-N-N-E-C-T-I-C-U-T! You know what a state is, don't you?"

"Nope," said Andrew.

"I can't believe it! You don't know anything!" I said.

"I do too know things. I know you're a sore winner!" said Andrew.

Luckily dinner was almost finished. I excused myself and went upstairs to study.

Later, Mommy came to say good night.

"Am I really a sore winner?" I asked.

"I'm afraid you have been a little bit," said Mommy. "It's nice to win. But winning isn't everything. Just like losing isn't everything.

You have to try not to be a sore winner *or* a sore loser."

"I'll try, Mommy," I said. We gave hugs and kisses. Then Mommy turned out the light.

I'll try hard not to be a sore winner, I thought. But I am *not* going to lose the next contest!

CHAPTER 6

I now declare Monday spelling bee day!" I said.

"Yay!" cried Nancy and Hannie.

Today was the spelling bee for the winners of each first-, second-, and third-grade class at Stoneybrook Academy.

Ms. Colman had told us on Friday that the spelling bee would be in the school auditorium. The room is blue. So this is what I wore:

— my blue-and-green-plaid skirt

— my blue sweater

— the plaid hair bow that Mommy gave me for my birthday.

I knew I looked great. Maybe even as great as Pamela, who gets dressed up all the time. But I still felt a little nervous. I had butterflies in my stomach. After all, everyone from three whole grades would be watching.

I decided to have a little talk with myself. Karen, you look great. You studied hard. Your best friends, Hannie and Nancy, are going to cheer you on. You are going to win this spelling bee! You are going to be the junior state champion!

"Spellers onstage," said Ms. Colman. "We are about to begin." (I was glad Ms. Colman was going to give us our words.)

This time I was the fourth speller. I was glad because the first three words were hard. But no one made any mistakes. These spellers were really good. Maybe even as good as me. But I was still going to win. Just as long as I didn't get careless.

"Karen, your word is *believe*," said Ms. Colman.

I knew that word. Seth had said, "You may not believe it, but there is a *lie* right in the middle of *believe*."

"Believe. B-E-L-I-E-V-E. Believe," I said.

"Yay!" called Nancy and Hannie.

"Okay, boys and girls. Please save your cheers for the end of the spelling bee," said Ms. Colman.

My stomach was starting to feel better. I could tell this was going to be easy, after all.

Before I knew it, two kids were out and my turn had come again. Then five kids were out. Then seven. Then just three of us were left.

"Karen, please spell *chimney*," said Ms. Colman.

Uh-oh. That was a hard one. When I was studying, I kept putting in an extra *e*. But where? I had to think.

"Karen? Did you hear the word?" asked Ms. Colman.

"Yes," I said. I looked at Hannie. She smiled at me. I smiled back. I was ready to spell the word.

"Chimney. C-H-I-M . . ." (Was this where the *e* went? I looked at Nancy. Then I remembered.

"The *m* and the *n* are together, just like in the alphabet," she had said.)

". . . N-E-Y! Chimney!" I said loud and clear.

"That is correct," said Ms. Colman.

Then, guess what! The next two kids missed their words! I was the winner! Yay!

I got a gift certificate for the Tall Tales Bookstore. And, I was going to be in the next spelling bee with all the other junior winners from the Stoneybrook schools.

"I'm the Queen Bee!" I cried when we got back to class. "Get it? The *Queen Bee*? The best?"

"No," said Pamela. "You're only the bee queen."

"She *is* the Queen Bee," said Hannie, coming to my rescue.

"You're just jealous of her," said Nancy.

Pamela did not answer. She sat at her desk.

"Karen's being a show-off," said Jannie and Leslie. And they went to their desks, just like Pamela.

"We are very proud of you," said Ms. Colman. "Let's all give Karen a round of applause."

Pamela, Jannie, and Leslie sat with their hands folded.

But who cared? Most of the kids clapped. And Ricky Torres even slipped me a note. Here's what it said:

To Karen, the Queen Bee, Bzzz. Bzzz. Bzzz. I'm glad you won, even if you are a show-off! Ricky, the King

CHAPTER 7

Boo. Boo. Boo! It was Tuesday. No spelling bee.

But I ended up having a good day anyway. Before we went home, Ms. Colman took me aside to tell me about the next spelling bee. I felt so, so important. I hoped Pamela was watching.

"The spelling bee will be held in two weeks, on a Monday night," said Ms. Colman. "It will be in the Stoneybrook High School auditorium. You may invite all the members of your family." (I think she said that on purpose because she knows how many members of my family there are.)

As soon as I got home, I showed Mommy the note.

"May I call Daddy and Kristy now?" I asked.

"You may call them after dinner," said Mommy.

I had a snack with Andrew. Then I went up to my room. I had important things to do. I closed the door. I took Emily Junior, my rat, out of her cage.

"How was your day?" I asked.

Sniff, sniff, sniff. Emily Junior doesn't talk, of course. Sometimes she races around. Sometimes she jumps into my shoe for a nap. That's what she did now.

Goosie, my stuffed cat, is always ready for a talk.

"I've got to decide what to wear for my big Monday night, Goosie. Will you help me?" I asked.

I made Goosie nod his head. Then I held him up to my ear.

"What color is the high school auditorium?" I repeated. Uh-oh. I forgot to ask. Maybe I should call Ms. Colman, I thought.

"What, Goosie? I don't have to match the

32

room? I should just wear my birthday hair bow? You're right! It was good luck."

The hair bow was green, red, and blue. I could wear my red sweater and my red-and-blue-plaid skirt.

"Thanks, Goosie!" I said. "Now I better start planning my acceptance speech. I don't want to look like a dweeb when I win!"

I sat Goosie and some of my other toys up on the dresser.

"You are the audience," I said.

Emily Junior was still sleeping in my shoe. I put her on my desk.

"You are Ms. Colman. You have just handed me my award," I said.

I put on my hair ribbon. Then I took a deep bow and said, "Thank you for this award! I am gigundo honored and proud to be the best junior speller in the state of Connecticut. As we all know, I am probably the best junior speller in the whole wide world!"

That should do it, I thought.

I waved to my audience and took one last bow.

CHAPTER 8

M-O-N-D-A-Y spells spelling day! The big spelling bee at Stoneybrook High was going to be tonight at seven-thirty. I decided to spell my way through the whole day!

"H-I, H-A-N-N-I-E!" I said when I saw Hannie. (I had already spelled hi to Nancy. Mommy had driven us to school.)

"H-I, K-A — Oh, forget it," said Hannie, giggling. "You're the one in the spelling bee. Not me."

"Please be seated everyone," said Ms. Colman. After attendance, Ms. Colman made the morning announcements. She saved the best for last.

"I have just learned that the state spelling bee

will be televised locally. That means if Karen wins tonight and goes on to the next contest, she might get to be on local TV."

I almost fell off my chair!

"Can you believe it?" I said to Ricky. (Ricky sits in the front row next to me. That's because we both wear glasses. We can see better up front.)

I got up and turned to look at Hannie and

Nancy. (They sit in the back of the room. They do not wear glasses.) We gave each other the thumbs-up sign.

All morning I studied my words — no matter what everyone else was studying.

"If John has four berries, in his basket, and Jill has six berries, how many berries do John and Jill have together?" asked Ms. Colman.

I knew the answer. It was ten. But ten wasn't on my list. So when Ms. Colman called on me I said, "E-L-E-V-E-N, take away one. That's ten!"

We studied geography later on. Ms. Colman pointed to a map.

"Who can tell me the name of this river?" she asked. I waved my arm like crazy. Ms. Colman called on me.

"M-I-S-S-I-S-S-I-P-P-I! It's the Mississippi River!" I said.

I heard someone groaning on the other side of the room. I was sure I knew who it was. Her initials are P. H.

At recess, I practiced for my television debut.

First I had to get my walk just right. This is what I did:

I threw back my head.

I took long, slow steps.

I twirled around to face my audience.

Then I smiled a great, big winner's smile!

"Thank you, thank you, thank you," I said to everyone on the playground. "It is so good to know that the whole state of Connecticut is watching me, the Queen Bee, on television tonight!"

"That's bee queen. And you haven't won yet. You could lose, you know," said Pamela.

"Why would I lose?" I said. "I don't plan on taking a Stupid Pill. So, L-A-D-I-E-S and G-E-N-T-L-E-M-E-N, thank you, thank you, thank you!"

Pamela stomped off to the other side of the yard. Jannie, Leslie, and a few other kids followed her.

That was okay. The Queen Bee — that's me — still had Hannie, Nancy, Ricky, and a few other kids on her side.

CHAPTER 9

This is it, Goosie," I said. "In a few hours, I will be onstage at Stoneybrook High School, spelling words."

Emily Junior rattled around in her cage.

"I'm sorry, Emily," I said. "I can't take you with me. But I'll tell you all about it when I get back."

It was time to get dressed. But first I had to do one thing. I had to make sure Daddy, Kristy, and everyone at the big house were coming to see me.

"Mommy, may I call Daddy?" I asked.

"You called him this afternoon," said Mommy.

"I need to call him again," I replied.

"All right, Karen. You may call Daddy," said Mommy.

"Thanks!" I cried. Nannie answered the phone. She said everyone was looking forward to seeing me later. I asked to talk to Daddy anyway.

"Hi, Daddy!" I said. "Are you coming tonight? Is *everyone* coming?"

"We'll all be there, Karen," said Daddy. "Even Emily Michelle."

"Well, I've got to get ready now, Daddy. See you later!" I said. I hung up the phone. I ran upstairs to get dressed.

I had changed my mind about what to wear. I had decided to wear pink. That was a happy color. I put on my pink shirt, pink skirt, pink socks, and pink hair bow. (I put my good luck birthday hair bow in my pocket.) Then I showed Mommy and Seth what I was wearing.

"You look lovely!" they said.

But when I saw myself in their mirror, I was not sure. I ran back to my room. This time I tried blue. Everything blue.

I showed Mommy and Seth again.

"What was the matter with the first outfit?" asked Seth.

"I'm not sure," I said. "Do you like *this* one?"

"Yes, I do," said Seth. "I like it very much."

"It's very nice," said Mommy.

But I *still* was not sure. Five outfits later, I was back to pink. I asked Mommy if I could call Daddy one more time.

"He told you he was coming, didn't he?" asked Mommy.

"Yes. But I have to tell him what I'm wearing, so he'll recognize me," I said. (I knew he would recognize me. But I needed to make sure nothing had happened since I had spoken to him.)

"All right. But this is the last time," said Mommy.

Daddy said pink sounded great.

I decided Andrew might need help getting dressed. It was important for him to look good. They might ask him to stand and take a bow when I won the contest.

"I don't need your help. Mommy showed me what to wear already," said Andrew.

I looked at the clothes on the bed. The shirt had a teeny tiny speck on it.

"That shirt has a big spot on it. I'll help you pick something else while you give me words," I said.

"OK!" said Andrew. "Spell *spell*."

"That's too easy. Give me something harder," I said.

"*Rock*! That's hard!" said Andrew. He threw himself on the bed, laughing.

I could see he was not going to be much help. So I picked out a new shirt for him and then found Mommy and Seth again.

"I need words," I said. I handed Seth the list.

"All right," said Seth. "Spell *mountain*."

"Mountain. M-O-U-N-T-A-I-N. Mountain," I said. "Now it's your turn, Mommy."

Mommy looked at the list. "Spell *joyous*," she said.

"Joyous. J-O-Y-O-U-S. Joyous," I said.

Andrew came into the room.

"How do I look?" he asked.

"Not now, Andrew. I'm spelling words," I said.

Andrew glared at me. "Mommy, how do you spell *pest*?" he asked.

"Pest. P-E-S-T. Pest," said Mommy.

Andrew and I stuck our tongues out at each other.

"It's time to go," said Seth.

We put on our coats and headed for the car.

By the time we were buckled up, I had already spelled *automobile*, *driveway*, *gasoline*, *engine*, and *highway*.

CHAPTER 10

I have never seen such a gigundo building!" I said.

"You've seen Stoneybrook High lots of times, Karen," said Seth. "I think it just looks bigger because you're nervous."

"Nervous? N-E-R-V-O-U-S? Nervous? Me? No way!" I said.

I was excited. I could hardly wait for the spelling bee to begin.

As soon as we found the auditorium, Ms. Colman waved to me. I had to go backstage with the other junior spelling bee winners right away. I was feeling important already!

"This is Mr. Monroe, a teacher from one of the other schools," said Ms. Colman. "He will be giving you your spelling words. Good luck, Karen!"

"If everyone will gather round me," said Mr. Monroe, "I will explain the rules."

I moved in closer so I could hear. I also wanted to check out the other kids. I could not tell much. They did not look especially smart, or dumb, or anything. Most everyone looked scared, though. I wondered if I did, too.

"This is how the spelling bee works," said Mr. Monroe. "I will give you a word. You say the word, spell it, then say it again. When you have finished spelling the word, I will tell you if you have spelled it correctly. If you have, remain standing where you are. If you have not spelled the word correctly, I will ask you to sit down. The next speller will have a chance to spell the same word. Any questions?"

No one had a question. Mr. Monroe gave us name tags. Then we went out onstage. The spelling bee was about to begin.

Luckily, Mr. Monroe had a few words to say

to the audience first. That gave me time to look for my families.

I found Mommy, Seth, and Andrew right away. They saw me and waved. But I could not find Daddy and the rest of my big-house family. My stomach flip-flopped. Then I saw Kristy waving. they were all there. Eight of them in one row!

"If the spellers are ready, we will begin now," said Mr. Monroe. "The first word is for you, Mark. Please spell *arithmetic*."

"Arithmetic. A-R-I-T-H-M-E-T-I-C. Arithmetic," said Mark.

"That is correct," said Mr. Monroe. "Paula, please spell *umbrella*."

"Umbrella. U-M-B-R-E-L-L-A. Umbrella," said Paula.

Guess whose turn was next. Mine. I was really nervous.

"Karen, please spell *separate*," said Mr. Monroe.

I thought, There is *a rat* in the middle of separate.

I spelled it. "Separate. S-E-P-A-R-A-T-E. Separate."

"That is correct," said Mr. Monroe.

I saw my families beaming. What a relief! Now that my first turn was over, maybe I could have some fun.

Mr. Monroe gave us more words. We spelled them. When kids got words wrong, they sat down. Soon just four of us were left.

"Lindsay, please spell *handkerchief*," said Mr. Monroe.

"Handkerchief. H-A-N-K-E-R-C-H-I-E-F. Hand-kerchief," said Lindsay.

"I'm sorry. That is not correct," said Mr. Monroe. "Mark, please spell *handkerchief.*"

"Handkerchief. H-A-N-D-K-E-R-C-H-E-I-F. Handkerchief," said Mark.

"I am sorry. That is not correct," said Mr. Monroe. "Paula, please spell *handkerchief.*"

"Handkerchief. H-A-N-D-K-E-C-H-I-E-F. Handkerchief," said Paula.

"I am sorry. That is not correct," said Mr. Monroe. "Karen, please spell *handkerchief.*"

"Handkerchief. H-A-N-D-K-E-R-C-H-I-E-F. Handkerchief," I said.

"Karen, that *is* correct. That makes you the winner of the Stoneybrook Junior Spelling Bee!" said Mr. Monroe.

I heard everyone clapping while Mr. Monroe shook my hand and gave me a $100 saving bond. "Use it well," he said.

I smiled at Mommy and Seth and Andrew and Daddy and Elizabeth and Kristy and Sam and Charlie and David Michael and Nanny and Emily Michelle! Yay! Hurray!

Someone closed the curtains before I had a chance to make my acceptance speech.

But guess what! An eighth-grader from Stoneybrook Academy interviewed me for the school paper. She even took my picture.

I was a star!

CHAPTER 11

Bye, Mrs. Dawes! Thank you for the ride!" I called. I raced out of Nancy's mom's car and into school.

"Wait for me!" called Nancy.

I couldn't wait. It was Tuesday. The day the *Stoneybrook Academy News* came out. I ran into the classroom.

I didn't see the paper, but I knew it would get there soon.

Ms. Colman was taking attendance when there was a knock at the door. An eighth-grader was carrying a stack of papers. He dropped them on Ms. Colman's desk. Since I sit in the first row, I got to see the front page.

So did Ms. Colman. "Congratulations, Karen," she said. "You may take the first copy."

Wow! I was headline news:

STONEYBROOK ACADEMY STUDENT TO ENTER FAIRFIELD COUNTY SPELLING BEE.

There was an article about the spelling bee inside. And my picture was right next to it!

"Look at this! I'm in the newspaper!" I called to everyone.

Ms. Colman gave our class time to read the article. Everyone was happy for me. Especially Hannie and Nancy. After all, we are the Three Musketeers. "One for all and all for one!" That is our motto.

But guess who acted like she didn't care. Pamela Harding.

"Show-off!" she said.

"That isn't fair," said Nancy. "The school reporter came to Karen. Karen didn't go to her."

"That's right," I said. "I didn't ask to be made a world-famous star."

Pamela would not even pick up the paper. Neither would Leslie or Jannie, or the rest of the kids who wanted to be Pamela's best friend.

But Ricky Torres was still my friend. He read the whole article.

"Congratulations, Karen," he said. Then he whispered, "But maybe you shouldn't shout so much about it."

"I think this calls for a celebration, class," said Ms. Colman. "It's not every day that one of your classmates makes front-page news.

On Friday afternoon, we will have a party in Karen's honor."

I saw Pamela roll her eyes. And I heard a few groans. But who cared? There was going to be a party in *my* honor!

CHAPTER 12

Work, lunch, recess, work . . . party!

That is how Friday went. Ms. Colman brought cookies and punch to school. And we were allowed to play board games.

Since the party was for me, I decided I should be the hostess. I tried out my new television walk.

"As you know, we are having this party because I am the best junior speller in Stoneybrook," I told a group of kids. I did not want them to forget why we were having the party in the first place. But I noticed that no one seemed to be listening to me.

"In fact," I said loud enough for Pamela to hear, "I may be the best junior speller in the whole country. Maybe even in the whole world!"

"If you were the best speller in the world, Miss Smarty-pants, you would have to know how to spell in French and Spanish and German and every single language there is," Pamela said.

"Ah, yes. You would be zee very good speller, *ma chérie*," Ricky said, trying to sound French. At least he was still being nice to me. But he was the only one.

Even Hannie and Nancy were ignoring me. They were playing Spill and Spell with Leslie and Jannie. They did not ask me to join them — and it is a spelling game!

I hated to admit it, but I was not having a good time at my own party. I wandered around the room. I ate some cookies and drank some punch. I tried talking to a few kids about the spelling bee. But I could tell they did not want to hear. I was sort of glad when the party was over.

When everyone was leaving, Ms. Colman asked if she could talk to me.

"I am very, very proud of how well you have been doing in these spelling bees, Karen," she said. "You have been studying hard and learning your words. But I think you need to learn another thing — what it means to be a good winner. A good winner does not boast and act more important than other people, Karen. A good winner shows humility and graciousness. Do you know those words, Karen?

"Humility? Sure! H-U-M-I-L-I-T-Y. Humility!"

I said. "And I know graciousness, too. G-R-A-C-I-O-U-S-N-E-S-S. Graciousness!" I spelled both words in about ten seconds.

I heard Ms. Colman give a little sigh.

"You may go now, Karen," she said.

"See you Monday!" I replied. And I ran out the door.

CHAPTER 13

It was a going-to-Daddy's Friday! When we pulled into the big-house driveway, Mommy called, "See you later, alligators!"

Daddy was waiting for us at the door.

"Look, Daddy!" I said, waving a copy of the *Stoneybrook Academy News* in front of him. "I'm on the front page!"

"Karen says she's an S-T-A-R, Daddy," Andrew said.

"I'm teaching Andrew how to spell. That's so he can follow in my famous footsteps," I said.

"Karen, hi!" called Kristy. "I want to see the paper, too," she said. Even though Kristy is thirteen and really busy with her Babysitters

Club, she always asks about things that happen to me. She is the greatest.

Everyone at the big house wanted to see the paper. While they were looking, I recited the article. I knew it by heart:

"'Karen Brewer entered and *won* last week's district' — that's D-I-S-T-R-I-C-T — 'junior spelling competition.

"'She now qualifies' —that's Q-U-A-L-I-F-I-E-S —'to enter the Fairfield County Spelling Bee.'"

I wanted to make sure everyone was listening. So I said, "Of course Karen Brewer, the world-famous superstar, will win that spelling bee, too. She will probably win every spelling bee she ever enters!"

"You're making that up!" said David Michael. "It doesn't say anything like that in there."

After dinner, Andrew, David Michael, and I played a game of Go Fish. Then Kristy read Moosie and me a chapter from my new book, *The Phantom Tollbooth*.

On Saturday morning, I popped out of bed.

I got dressed and had breakfast. Hannie was coming over early to play.

Ding-dong! Ding-dong! There she was! It was raining, so we went upstairs to my room to play.

"Want to make paper dolls? I brought pretty construction paper," said Hannie.

"Wow! Construction. What a neat word. I might be asked to spell it at the state contest. C-O-N-S-T-R-U-C-T-I-O-N. Construction. Did I get it right?"

"I guess so," said Hannie. "Do you want to make dolls or not?"

"Sure," I said. I got out my crayons.

"Pass the red crayon, please," said Hannie.

"How about this one! Magenta. M-A-G-E-N-T-A. Magenta," I spelled. "Or maybe you want sepia. S-E-P-I-A. Sepia."

"Cut it out, Karen," said Hannie. "I'm tired of listening to you spell words all the time."

"Cut it out?" I said. "Wait just a minute and I'll get my scissors. Get it? Cut? Scissors? S-C-I-S-S-O-R-S. Scissors."

I thought my joke was pretty funny. But Hannie did not. I changed the subject.

"I am definitely going to win the two-hundred-and-fifty-dollar grand prize at the state contest. What do you think I should do with it?" I asked.

"I think you should give me half of it for listening to you spell all day," said Hannie.

"Maybe I'll take a long trip around the world," I said. "I'll send you postcards from all the exotic — that's E-X —"

"Karen, *stop*," said Hannie.

I did not really feel like making dolls. I wanted to pick out what I would wear to the state contest. After all, I was going to be on TV! I tried on my blue corduroy jumper.

"What do you think of this?" I asked Hannie.

"It's fine," she said.

I tried on my green sweater with the pink bows on it.

"Is this better?" I asked Hannie.

"It's fine, too," she said. But she didn't even look up.

I tried a few more outfits.

"Do you like this?" I asked. "Will it look good on TV?"

"I don't care, Karen Brewer! You don't want to play with me. All you want to do is talk about the silly spelling contests. I'm leaving!" said Hannie.

She left in a huff. She even slammed the door.

I was sorry she was mad. But I had important things to do.

CHAPTER 14

Something was wrong. When I got to school Monday morning, Hannie and Nancy were talking with Pamela, Jannie, and Leslie.

They were all laughing together. You would think they were the Five Musketeers or something.

I went through the whole morning without saying a word to anyone, not even Ricky. And he sits right next to me.

By recess, I was about to burst. I ran out with my hopscotch stone, ready for a game with Hannie and Nancy. Even if they had been mad at me this morning, I figured they would be over it by now.

They weren't. They were hanging around with Pamela again.

"Want to play hopscotch?" I asked. I was asking Hannie and Nancy. Not Pamela.

"How come you're not spelling everything this morning?" asked Hannie. "I thought that's what bee queens do."

"It's Queen Bee," I said. "And you are being a toad."

"You haven't played hopscotch with us in days. All you do is walk around like you're a television star," said Nancy.

"Some friends you are," I said. "I thought we were the Three Musketeers. One for all and all for one."

"We *were* the Three Musketeers," said Nancy. "Now we're the *Two* Musketeers — me and Hannie. Unless Pamela wants to join us. Then we'll be three again."

Pamela was smiling a lot. I could see she was really enjoying this. That made me so mad.

"You're all just jealous," I said. "But you'll

be sorry when I win my two hundred and fifty dollars. If I had good friends, I'd do nice things for them with my money. First I'd take them to a fancy restaurant. They could order *anything* they wanted. Then we'd go to the movies. I'd buy the tickets. And I'd buy the popcorn and soda, too."

"Big deal," said Nancy. "You can't *buy* friends, you know. You have to make them — and keep them."

"That's right," said Hannie. "Friends play

with each other. They don't act like big shots all the time, spelling dumb words and trying on clothes."

"I'll go to the movies with you," said Ricky. "But don't you think you should win the spelling bee first?"

"Don't worry. I'll win," I said. "But when I do, I'm not buying anything for anybody!"

I stomped off to play hopscotch by myself. It had *not* been a good day.

CHAPTER 15

It was Friday night. I was in my room in the little house. I was all ready for the County Contest.

"Wish me luck, Emily Junior. You, too, Goosie," I said.

Sniff. Sniff. I knew that was rat talk for good luck.

I made Goosie give me a big kiss. "Thanks, Goosie," I said.

Mommy and Seth and Andrew and I drove to the Stamford Assembly Hall. That is where the contest was going to be held. My big-house family was going to be there, too.

The Assembly Hall is giant. I could have

asked Hannie and Nancy to come to the contest. But I did not. Not after they had been so mean to me.

"Are you feeling all right, Karen?" asked Mommy.

"Yes," I said. But I was feeling very nervous. My stomach was jumping all over the place. And even though I was mad at them, I missed Hannie and Nancy. I would have felt better if I had known that they would be at the Assembly Hall to cheer me on.

"Couldn't Hannie or Nancy come tonight?" asked Seth.

"No," I said. I did not feel like telling anyone that they were mad at me. And that they probably did not even care if I won or lost tonight. That was the worst part of all.

When we reached the Assembly Hall, Ms. Colman called me backstage. She introduced me to Ms. Matthews. Ms. Matthews said the rules were the same as before.

The kids that were backstage with me were the best spellers in their districts. I was getting more and more nervous. What if I did not win? I *had* to win.

All I had to do was concentrate.

Ms. Matthews stepped up to the front of the stage. "Good evening, ladies and gentlemen," she said. "Welcome to the county spelling contest. As you know, tonight's winner will go on to the state contest. May the best speller win!"

It was time for us to walk onto the stage.

The spelling bee began.

"Martin, please spell *gnome*," said Ms. Matthews.

"Gnome. G-N-O-M-E. Gnome," said Martin.

"That is correct," said Ms. Matthews.

What a relief! If I had been given that word I would have gotten it wrong! I would have spelled it N-O-M-E.

The words were hard. And these spellers were good. By the time Ms. Matthews got to me, I was really scared.

"Karen, please spell *anticipate*," said Ms. Matthews.

I knew this word. All I had to do was *concentrate*.

"Anticipate," I said. "A-N-T —"

Wah! Wah! Wah! I would know that sound anywhere! It was Emily Michelle crying. I looked up and saw Charlie rushing her out of the auditorium. Oh, no!

"Please begin again," said Ms. Matthews.

I took a deep breath and started over.

"Anticipate. A-N-T-I-C-I-P-A-T-E. Anticipate," I said.

"That is correct," said Ms. Matthews.

The spelling bee seemed to go on forever. I was getting tired. I was having trouble concentrating. But so were the other kids. They were making a lot of mistakes. Before I knew it, only three of us were left. After that, the end went fast.

A girl named McKenzie spelled *dictionary*

wrong. Then I heard Ms. Matthews saying, "I'm sorry, Martin. That is not correct. Karen, please spell *dictionary*."

This is my chance, I thought. If I spell this right, I get to be in the state contest. I have *got* to do it!

"Dictionary. D-I-C-T-I-O-N-A-R-Y. Dictionary," I said.

"Karen, that is correct. Congratulations! You are the winner of the county spelling bee," said Ms. Matthews. "Now you will go on to the *state* contest!"

Hurray! I got another $100 savings bond. And a real reporter from a real newspaper interviewed me.

"We'd like to get your picture, too, if you don't mind," said a photographer.

I smiled for the camera. "Thanks," said the reporter. "You will be able to read the story in several county papers, including the *Stoneybrook News.*"

I raced to the auditorium. My big-house and little-house families were together, all hugging me at once.

"Yay!" cried Emily Michelle.

Emily Michelle was being pretty cute. And nice. But I was tired. And I was a little mad at her.

"You almost ruined everything!" I said. "You almost made me lose the contest."

Emily began to cry.

CHAPTER 16

By the time I got to school on Monday, I was feeling better.

"Karen, we are proud of you for winning the county spelling contest," said Ms. Colman.

"Thank you," I said. I tried not to make too big a deal out of it. I did not jump up and down like before. I did not even say anything about my picture being in the paper again.

"Let's give Karen a round of applause," Ms. Colman said.

Ricky clapped for me loudly. "Way to go!" he said. I guess he had forgotten that I had even been a little mean to *him*.

I turned around to see if Nancy and Hannie were clapping, too. Guess what! They were! Not a lot. But it was still a good sign. I guess they did care, even though they were mad at me.

At recess, I grabbed my hopscotch stone. On my way to the playground I said to myself over and over, I will not say a single word about spelling. I will not say a single word about spelling. I will not say —

"Here comes the ex-Musketeer," Hannie whispered to Nancy.

I made believe I did not hear her.

"Hi. Want to play hopscotch with me?" I asked.

Hannie and Nancy did not answer right away. They turned their backs and started whispering again.

When they turned around, Nancy said, "We'll only play with you if you promise not to start spelling everything, Miss Bee Queen."

"I promise!" I said.

We sang *Eeny meeny miny mo* to see who went first. Nancy won. That was okay with me. I was just happy to be playing.

"I've got an idea! Let's have a hopscotch contest," I said.

"Oh, brother! Not every game is a *contest*," said Nancy.

"That's right," said Hannie. "I've changed my mind. I don't want to play with you after all."

"Me, neither," said Nancy.

I must have said the wrong thing. They were mad at me all over again. I knew they would not listen to me now. No matter what.

So I went to the library. I took down the dictionary. I was going to study some big words. But there were two easy words I wanted to look up first. One was *contest*.

contest: 1. A struggle for victory between competitors. 2. Any competition, especially one rated by judges.

The other word was *win*.

win: 1. To achieve victory over others in a competition. 2. To achieve success in an effort or venture.

That is what I was going to do in the spelling contest. Win! I still wanted to be the best junior

speller in the state of Connecticut. I wanted that
badly.

I had a lot of studying to do.

CHAPTER 17

I could not believe it! It was Friday. The night of the big state contest! I was going to be on TV!

I was glad it was a big-house weekend. That meant Kristy could help me get ready.

Mommy had bought me a brand-new dress just for the contest. It was blue with white trim and gold buttons.

I put it on and Kristy helped me button it. Of course, I had to wear my good luck birthday hair ribbon. Kristy helped me tie it just right.

"You look great," said Kristy. She paused. Then she said, "You know, I haven't heard you say anything about Hannie and Nancy. Aren't they coming?"

I did not want to talk about the Two Musketeers. But I do not like keeping secrets from Kristy.

"No. They're not coming. They're mad at me. They think I talk too much about contests," I said.

"I'm sorry," said Kristy. "But I'm sure you three will make up soon. Listen, I've got to get dressed now. Call if you need me."

After Kristy left, I twirled around in front of the mirror.

"How do I look, Moosie?" I asked. "Do you think I look like a spelling-bee winner? Really? And a TV star, too? Thanks!"

Ring! Ring!

"Your mom's on the phone, Karen," called Charlie a moment later.

I dashed for the upstairs phone.

"Hi, Mommy! . . . Yes. I'm all ready. And I love my new dress. Are you leaving now? . . . Okay. I'll see you there!" I said.

Everyone in the big house was ready. They

were very dressed up. I was gigundo glad because I knew the reporters would want to talk to them after I won the contest. They would want to ask my family how I got to be such a great speller.

We had to drive two cars to the state capital because there were so many of us. I rode with Daddy, Elizabeth, Kristy, David Michael, and Andrew. Nannie took Sam, Charlie, and Emily Michelle in her old, clunky car, the Pink Clinker. (Sam and Charlie think the Pink Clinker is so, so embarrassing. I like it!)

It was a long drive. Daddy said it would take about an hour and a half to get to Hartford. That is where the state spelling bee would be held.

Elizabeth tried telling stories and singing songs in the car. But that did not help. I was nervous the whole time. And I was worried that the Pink Clinker would not make it.

But it did!

"Hi, Ms. Colman!" I called when we entered the TV studio. Boy, was I glad to see her.

"Hi, Karen. Come on. I'll show you where to go," she said.

"Good luck, honey," said Daddy. "I know you'll do your best, and that's good enough for us."

Everyone gave me lots of hugs and kisses. Then they went to find seats. I did not have time to look for Mommy and Seth. Ms. Colman said I had to hurry. I would find them later.

We went to a place called the greenroom. That is what they call the room in a television studio where all the important guests wait. And I was a very important guest!

A man named Mr. Gregory was in charge of the spelling bee. He seemed nice. He reminded us what the rules were. I already knew them by heart. So I studied the competition. Four boys and three girls. Too bad they were all going to lose. But only one person could win this contest. And that person was going to be me!

We waited in the greenroom while everyone in the audience got settled. For once in my life,

I did not feel like talking. I wanted to practice spelling in my head.

I was in the middle of spelling *independence* (four *e*'s, no *a*'s) when a girl came up to me and introduced herself.

"Hi, I'm Melissa. What's your name?" she said.

"Karen. But I can't talk now. I'm studying," I said. I did not mean to be rude. But I really was studying.

"I've been studying hard, too. I want to win

this contest so much," said Melissa. "Spelling is just about the only thing I'm good at. And now the kids in school think I'm really important. So I've just got to win tonight."

I wondered why she was telling me this. Didn't she know that *I* was going to win?

CHAPTER 18

It was eight o'clock sharp. We were all onstage. There were cameras and lights everywhere. It was really hot under the lights. And they were so bright. At first I could not see the audience.

But then my eyes got used to the lights. I picked out both my families right away. They were all smiling at me.

I was wearing a banner that said, FAIRFIELD. (That's the county in Connecticut where I live.) I felt like I was in a beauty pageant or a talent contest.

"Good evening ladies and gentlemen in our audience. Television viewers. Welcome to the Junior State Spelling Bee!" said Mr. Gregory.

"Before we begin, I would like to tell you how our spelling bee is going to work. . . ."

Oh, good, I thought. I could figure out how long it would take me to win. There were seven other spellers. I would give them each about three chances to make a mistake. If each mistake took a minute or so, in about twenty minutes, I would be the true Queen Bee!

"Are you ready, spellers?" asked Mr. Gregory.

We were ready. A boy named Stanley had the first turn.

"Stanley, please spell *stallion*," said Mr. Gregory.

"Stallion. S-T-A-L-L-I-O-N. Stallion," said Stanley.

"That is correct," said Mr. Gregory.

That was just the beginning. Everyone got the first word right. My word was *royalty*. That is what I was going to feel like when I won.

Then everyone got their second word right, too. And their third. It was twenty minutes before anyone made a mistake. These kids were good!

Stanley missed *management*. (He left out the first *e*.) A girl named Michelle missed *pumpkin*. (She forgot the second *p*.)

Melissa did not miss any words. And neither did I. Finally, we were the only ones left. It was just like Nancy and me in the very first spelling bee. Back and forth, back and forth for ten minutes straight. Melissa spelled *thermometer*. I spelled *galoshes*. Melissa spelled *magician*. I spelled *proudly*.

I knew it would not be long now before Melissa made a mistake. Just like Nancy. I started thinking about my acceptance speech. And the trip to Washington I would take in six months to be in the *national contest*! Ms. Colman had told me about that in the greenroom.

"Karen, please spell *convertible*," said Mr. Gregory.

"Convertible. C-O-N-V-E-R-T-A-B-L-E. Convertible," I said.

"I'm sorry, Karen. That was incorrect," said Mr. Gregory.

What?! No way. I knew that word! I went back over what I had said. C-O-N-V-E-R-T-A — Oh, no! It is spelled with an *i*, not an *a*!

"Melissa, if you can spell *convertible* correctly, you will be our state winner," said Mr. Gregory.

"Convertible. C-O-N-V-E-R-T-I-B-L-E. Convertible," said Melissa.

She got it right! She had won!

"Congratulations, Melissa," said Mr. Gregory. "You are our state champion!"

CHAPTER 19

Thank you! Thank you so much!" said Melissa. I could see how excited she was.

Melissa turned to me. "I'm sorry you missed," she said. And she shook my hand. I think that is what Ms. Colman would have called being gracious.

I decided it was time for me to try being gracious, too.

"Congratulations," I said.

I watched Melissa accept the check for $250. And she got a certificate signed by the governor.

I got a certificate also. "Thank you," I said. I shook Mr. Gregory's hand. I even managed to smile.

The next thing I knew, the television cameras were rolling in for close-up pictures of Melissa. The reporters were crowding around her.

"Will you be able to come to the national contest in Washington, DC?" asked one of the reporters.

"Oh, yes!" said Melissa.

There was no reason for me to be onstage anymore. I saw Ms. Colman in the wings. I saw Mommy and Seth in the auditorium.

"Karen, I hope you don't feel too bad. You did very well," said Ms. Colman, when I had left the stage.

Mommy and Seth put their arms around me.

"We're sorry you didn't win. We know how much you wanted to be the best state speller," said Mommy.

"But we're very proud of you," added Seth.

"I'll pick you and Andrew up on Sunday night," said Mommy.

Then everyone from the big house crowded around me. They hugged and kissed me just

as much as when I had been the winner of the county contest.

"Can we go home now?" I asked Daddy.

"Sure," said Daddy. "Do you feel like stopping for ice cream on the way?"

"I don't think so. I'm pretty tired," I said.

"Maybe we'll have a treat tomorrow, then," said Elizabeth. "You came so far in the spelling bees. We have to celebrate sometime."

"You looked great up there, Karen," said Kristy. "I was so proud of my little sister."

All of a sudden I felt like crying. My eyes started to fill up.

"We'll talk more when we get home," whispered Kristy. She knew I did not want everyone to see that I was upset.

"I still think you're an S-T-A-R," said Andrew, looking proud of himself.

"Nice going, Professor," said David Michael.

Everyone had something nice to say. Even Emily Michelle.

"Yay!" she cried again.

She did not understand at all.

CHAPTER 20

By the time we got back to the big house it was almost midnight. Elizabeth brought a glass of milk and some cookies to my room. I think she knew I did not want to sit downstairs in the kitchen.

I put on my pajamas quickly and called Kristy to come tuck me in.

I sat up in bed, with Moosie next to me. Kristy sat down beside us.

"How are you feeling?" Kristy asked.

"Okay, I guess. On the way home, I was thinking hard. I decided maybe I deserved to lose. Because I was such a sore winner. But I really do hate being a loser."

"First of all, you should not call yourself a *loser*," said Kristy. "Tell me, how many spelling contests were you in?"

"Let's see," I said. I counted on my fingers. "There was one in class. One in school. One at the high school. The country spelling bee. And the one tonight. That's five."

"And how many did you win?" asked Kristy.

Again, I counted on my fingers. "One, two, three, four." I said. "Hey! That's pretty good!"

"Now, how many kids were in this last contest?" asked Kristy.

I was starting to get the idea. "Eight!" I said. "And I won second place! Second place in all of Connecticut!"

"So, remember, you are not a loser," said Kristy. "And you have your prize to prove it — a certificate from the governor."

Kristy was right. I was a winner after all. I decided that feeling like a winner was a pretty neat prize, too.

"Now, tell me how you were a *sore* winner," said Kristy.

"Well, I've been acting like I was better than everyone. I called myself the Queen Bee. I went around spelling things all day. And I wouldn't listen to anyone else, not even my best friends," I said.

"That's being a sore winner, all right!" said Kristy. But I could see she wasn't mad. She was smiling. "What are you going to do about it now?" she asked.

I had to think for a moment.

"Apologize?" I suggested.

"That sounds like a good idea," said Kristy.

"You know what makes me mad, though?" I said. "I *knew* how to spell *convertible*. I really did."

"I know. I've heard you spell it before. But that's all right. Maybe you'll get another chance next year. And I'll help you practice," said Kristy.

"Promise?" I asked, yawning.

"Promise," said Kristy.

I snuggled down under the covers with Moosie. Kristy gave both of us butterfly kisses with her eyelashes. "Good night, Karen," she said.

"Good night, Kristy. That's K-R-I-S-T-Y. Kristy," I said. We both started giggling. Then Kristy left and my room was quiet.

I practiced on Moosie what I was going to say to Hannie and Nancy.

"So, Hannie and Nancy. Do you think you can forgive me for being a show-off?" I asked.

I made Moosie nod his head to say yes. I really did think they would forgive me. Maybe not right away. But soon.

After all, we are the Three Musketeers!

About the Author

Ann M. Martin's The Baby-sitters Club has sold over 190 million copies and inspired a generation of young readers. Her novels include the Newbery Honor Book *A Corner of the Universe*, *A Dog's Life*, and the Main Street series. She lives in upstate New York.

Keep reading for a sneak peek at the next
Baby-sitters Little Sister book!

Karen's Ghost

Kristy, do I really have to go to sleep now?" I
asked my big sister.

"Yes, you do. It's already past your bedtime."

I sighed. Kristy is one of my favorite people
in the whole wide world. But she is thirteen.
And when she says to do something, you have
to do it. Besides, Kristy was my baby-sitter
that night. And you have to listen to baby-sitters,

just like you have to listen to teachers and mommies and daddies and grandparents and policemen.

"One more story?" I begged.

Kristy shook her head. "You already had one more story. And before that you had three stories."

"Yeah," I said, smiling. "And all of them were about Halloween."

"Are you going to be able to sleep tonight?" Kristy asked me.

"Sure," I replied. "Witches and ghosts don't scare me." (That was easy to say when the light was on and Kristy was sitting next to me.)

"All right," said Kristy. She sounded a little uncertain. "Under the covers, then. I hope you have good dreams tonight."

Kristy stood up, and I slid under my covers. I scrunched up my pillow.

"Don't forget to turn on my night-light," I said.

Kristy switched on my special light from

Disney World. Then she kissed me good night, turned off my lamp, and headed for the door.

"Leave the door open a crack!" I called.

"Okay." Kristy left my room.

I was alone.

I looked around. I was glad the night-light was on and the door was open.

Halloween was coming. That was why I wanted to hear all the Halloween stories. I just love Halloween. I love ghosts and witches, too. But I will tell you something. They *do* scare me a little bit. But that is only because a real witch lives next door. And a ghost lives upstairs and haunts his room on the third floor of our house. He haunts the attic, too.

The witch is named Morbidda Destiny. Well, that's what *I* call her. It's her witch name. Most people call her Mrs. Porter, but they don't know anything. Morbidda Destiny holds witch meetings at her house. At night, she flies around on a broomstick. (Adults do not believe this.)

I sat up and looked out my window. Morbidda Destiny's broomstick was leaning next to her front door. I could see it by the porch light. I guessed she wasn't going to go out haunting that night.

I lay down again. I listened.

CREEEEAK. What was that? Was it Ben Brewer?

I felt gigundo scared. Ben Brewer is the ghost in my house. I am not sure if he ever drifts below the third floor. What if he does? What if he was in my room *right then* . . . watching me?

"Go away, Ben Brewer," I whispered. "You can't scare me."

CREEEEAK.

"Honest," I said. "You can't scare me." But my voice was shaking.

I sat up and checked out the window again. Morbidda Destiny's porch light was off! Was her broom still there? Was she out haunting?

I almost called for Kristy. Then I remembered

that I had told her that witches and ghosts don't scare me.

I tried to think about other things. First I thought about Kristy. She is my stepsister. That's because my daddy married her mommy. See, I have two families. . . .

Don't miss any of the books in the Baby-sitters Little Sister series by Ann M. Martin—available as ebooks

Want more baby-sitting?

And many more!

DON'T MISS
THE BABY-SITTERS CLUB
GRAPHIC NOVELS!